Trapped!

Zeke turned as he ran. When he saw how close the astronomer was, he picked up his pace. Cassie could barely keep up with him. Her only hope was that Trexler was in worse shape than she was. Come on, feet, she thought. Run!

They flew down one street and up another, around corners and over lawns. Finally, Zeke made a sharp turn into an overgrown backyard. Cassie followed a moment later—and quickly screeched to a halt. Zeke was standing still, staring up at a fence that was at least ten feet high. There was no way out.

Look for the next exciting book in the series
The Spy from Outer Space:

Escape from Earth

Coming soon!

TOO MANY SPIES

Debra Hess

Illustrated by Carol Newsom

Hyperion Paperbacks for Children
New York

Produced by Chardiet Unlimited, Inc., 33 West 17th Street,
New York, New York 10011.
A Hyperion Paperback original
First edition: September 1993

1   3   5   7   9   10   8   6   4   2

Library of Congress Cataloging-in-Publication Data

Hess, Debra
Too many spies/Debra Hess—1st ed.
p.   cm.—(The spy from outer space)
Summary: Zeke, an alien boy stranded on Earth, continues to pose
as a human with the aid of ten-year-old Super Sleuth Cassie
Williams while trying to discover the identity of the mysterious man
who is following him. Sequel to *Alien Alert*.
ISBN 1-56282-569-0
[1. Extraterrestrial beings—Fiction.   2. Science fiction.]
I. Title.   II. Series: Hess, Debra.   Spy from outer space.
PZ7.H4326To   1993
[FIC]—dc20   95-529
CIP
AC

For Bernice,
who believes in me

TOO MANY SPIES

CHAPTER

In the dim light of dawn, Super Sleuth Cassie Williams crouched behind a massive oak tree, plucked the ray gun from her spy belt, held her breath, and waited. She strained to hear the sound of footsteps crunching the dead autumn leaves. But the woods were strangely silent.

Suddenly a loud crack split the air. Cassie jumped to her feet, turned, and pressed the trigger on her gun. A golden ray of light shot out into the hazy shadows. For a split second, Cassie could see massive trees, tangled vines—and the fallen branch that lay across her path. The cracking sound had simply been the heavy branch breaking. Cassie let her breath out slowly.

He had been right behind her—this spy from the Interstellar Spy Academy. He was swift. He was clever. And he was getting too close for comfort. If she could just get behind him, just get one good shot . . .

Cassie slipped out from behind the tree and started running. A hundred yards from the edge of the woods, she heard the footsteps she'd been expecting. She froze, then turned and took aim.

The footsteps came faster. Cassie squinted into the darkness but saw nothing. Her palms were sweating so heavily, she was afraid the gun would slip out of her hand. The sound of dried leaves crackling got louder and louder.

Then suddenly someone—or something—leapt from overhead, tackling Cassie to the ground.

"Uncle! Uncle!" Cassie cried.

"What does 'uncle' mean?" a boy's voice asked.

"It means I give up," said Cassie. "You win, Zeke. Get off of me."

Zeke laughed and helped Cassie to her feet. She brushed the dirt off her clothes and followed her friend to a clearing nearby. Once there, Zeke removed a small device from his pocket, pointed it directly in front of him, and pressed a button.

Immediately, a golden glow filled the clearing. As it grew larger and larger, it began to take on a rounded shape. In less than thirty seconds, an enormous golden spaceship stood before them.

"I'm glad you fixed the invisibility shield," said Cassie.

"Spot accomplished the actual repair," said Zeke. He pressed another button on the gadget in his hand and a staircase descended from the ship. The two friends clambered up the steps.

Once on board, Zeke reactivated the spaceship's invisibility shield, then filled two glasses with a red liquid. Carrying them to the table, he sat down beside his favorite Earthling.

"You should not have moved from behind that tree," he said. "I had lost track of you. I would never have found you there."

"I know," Cassie sighed. "But a branch broke off behind me and I panicked."

She fingered the ray gun on the table in front of her. "I can't believe this is just a toy."

"Actually, it is an instructional device used for training the spies of the Interstellar Spy Academy," said Zeke.

"Right," said Cassie. "It's a toy."

"I will be issued a real ray gun upon graduation," Zeke said proudly. He paused. "That is, if I ever get back to school."

Cassie heard a sigh escape at the end of Zeke's sentence and knew that her alien friend was feeling homesick. She couldn't blame him.

After all, Zeke and his parents, Mirac and Inora, never expected to be here at all. They had been traveling from their planet, Triminica, to the vacation planet, Clurigan, when their ship's computer had malfunctioned and sent them plummeting to Earth. Cassie had been looking through the night-vision periscope from her Super Deluxe Spy Kit at the exact moment the ship entered the earth's atmosphere. So far, she was the only one in Hillsdale who knew there were Triminicans on earth.

At least, she hoped she was.

"You'll get back to your planet, Zeke," she said. "Meanwhile, you can keep teaching me how to be a real spy. That game was fun. Scary, but fun."

"It is better on the third moon of Sargony," said Zeke. "The forest is darker and denser there."

Cassie grinned at him. It was great to have a friend who loved spying as much as she did.

"The only thing I don't understand," she said, thinking back to the game, "is how come I heard those footsteps in front of me and then you jumped from the tree behind me?"

Zeke grinned. "I cheated," he said.

"Cheated!" cried Cassie. "How?"

"I used Spot. He did the running, and I hid up in the tree."

Spot was Zeke's robot. Or rather, "Spot" was the name Zeke and Cassie had given the alien's robot when they first disguised him as a dog. All of the Triminicans had agreed to make changes in order to blend into life on Earth. They spoke English, wore wigs to cover their baldness, and clipped their foot-long fingernails. It was true that Spot had the worst of it, though. He didn't enjoy behaving like a dog one little bit. But the robot understood that if the Triminicans were going to keep their identity a secret, they would have to look like Earth creatures.

"The time for departure has arrived," droned a voice just then. A metal creature covered in wigs appeared in the room.

"Thanks, Spot," said Cassie, picking up her knapsack. She stood up from the table and grinned at Zeke.

"Can we use a materializer disk?"

"No," Spot answered. "Mirac has forbidden it."

"Yeah, well, Mirac isn't here," said Cassie.

"Actually," said Zeke, standing up from the table and facing the robot, "Mirac just said we should be careful of being *seen* using the disks."

"His exact words were 'Exercise extreme caution when utilizing materializer disks. Choose

Earth transportation when possible,'" droned Spot.

"Exactly!" said Cassie. "We have no Earth transportation."

"You have feet," said Spot.

Cassie squinted at the robot. "Was that humor?" she asked.

"No," said Spot.

Cassie laughed.

"School commences in exactly twenty-two minutes," warned Spot, moving toward the ship's exit.

"We're leaving," said Zeke. "Keep the invisibility shield on. And do not leave the ship for any reason."

The robot did not object.

Zeke and Cassie descended the steps of the ship and started walking to school.

"It's almost like the robot really has feelings," said Cassie, shivering in the early autumn air.

"What do you mean?" asked Zeke.

"Well," said Cassie, "the first time we went to school, Spot insisted on following us. There was nothing you could say to convince him to stay on the ship. Now it's like he remembers what happened to him and he's afraid it will happen again."

Zeke kicked at a pile of leaves in front of him but remained silent. Cassie knew he was thinking about Spot. The first time the Triminicans had landed on Earth, Mirac and Inora had left Zeke in Spot's care while they went to a Hawaiian island in search of iridium—a substance needed to create the ship's fuel. Their search had been successful. But by the time Zeke's parents returned, the robot had been captured by the local dogcatcher, locked in the Hillsdale Zoo, and beaten up by a gorilla. Poor Spot.

"That is memory, not emotion," Zeke said finally. But he didn't sound too sure.

"Well, whatever it is," said Cassie, "that robot definitely doesn't want to leave the ship."

"At least this time the invisibility shield is operative," said Zeke. "No one will see the ship even if they wander into the clearing."

They rounded a corner, and Hillsdale Elementary School loomed in front of them. Cassie stopped walking and touched Zeke's arm.

"Zeke?" she said softly.

Zeke stopped, too, and looked at her.

"I'm sorry your ship landed back on Earth again. But I'm really glad you're here."

Zeke smiled.

"I am also pleased to be spending more time with you, Cassie," he said.

Cassie smiled to herself. She had gotten used

to the formal way that Zeke spoke. She knew their friendship meant as much to him as it did to her.

"I do hope Mirac and Inora can locate more iridium though," said Zeke. "We are not meant to live on this planet."

"Even if they do find the iridium, didn't Mirac say that something pulled the ship down again?" asked Cassie.

"Yes, unfortunately," said Zeke. "We cannot take off again until we identify and correct that problem."

The school bell rang in the distance. Zeke and Cassie looked at each other and broke into a run. As they raced up the steps to the building, a large boy stepped into their path.

"I've been looking for you," he snarled at Zeke.

"It appears that you have found me," said Zeke.

"Three o'clock. The playground." The boy slammed his right fist into the palm of his left hand and stormed into the school.

Cassie rolled her eyes at Zeke and groaned. Ben O'Brien was the bully of the fifth grade. Zeke was the only person ever to beat him at Laser Lunacy, the most difficult game at the Hillsdale arcade. Losing the contest had embarrassed Ben in front of half the school, and afterward he had threatened to beat up the alien, who he believed was Cassie's cousin. Cassie and Zeke had not taken the threats seriously, since they had assumed Zeke would be back on his home planet by now.

"It looks like I will have to fight the bully after all," Zeke said.

Cassie sighed.

"It sure does," she said. "Do you know how to fight?"

"I have some fighting skills at my command," said Zeke. "But I would rather not use them unless absolutely necessary. I do not want to call attention to myself."

"You may not have a choice," said Cassie.

"I will attempt verbal communication first," said Zeke.

Cassie laughed. "You're going to try to talk to Ben? Good luck!"

The second bell rang. The two friends raced through the doors of the school.

In a corner of the school yard, a man wearing wire-rimmed glasses glanced at a photograph in his hand and smiled.

By five minutes after three, a crowd had gathered on the playground. Word of the challenge had gotten around, and everyone wanted to see if Zeke, the new boy, would show up.

Zeke was there.

Ben was not.

Marilee Tischler was being her usual sickening self.

"Zeke, you're the only boy in school who has the nerve to stand up to Ben," she oozed in her sticky-sweet voice.

Cassie groaned. Marilee Tischler had always been the most stuck-up, perfectly dressed, perfectly obnoxious girl in her class. Over the summer she stole Cassie's best friend, Melinda. Then, to make things worse, Marilee discovered flirting. If there was anything Cassie could do about it, Marilee was not going to steal Zeke away from her, too.

"Leave Zeke alone, Marilee," said Cassie. "He has to prepare for the fight."

"I need no preparation," said Zeke. "I will not fight him. I detest physical violence."

"But if you do fight him, I just know you'll win," cooed Marilee.

Zeke smiled at her. "Ben is clumsy and full of anger," he said. "It is true that I have the advantage."

"So, Zeke, there's something I've been wanting to ask you," Marilee went on in her sweetest voice. "There's a science competition coming up at school, and you have to have a partner to enter."

"So I have heard," said Zeke.

"And the teams are supposed to be boy-girl."

Cassie groaned.

Marilee glared at her but continued talking. "I was wondering if you'd like to be my partner, Zeke."

"He's already got a partner," Cassie said quickly.

Zeke glanced at her. Cassie thought he looked amused.

"Oh, really?" snapped Marilee. "Who?"

"Me!" Cassie snapped back.

"I want to hear it from Zeke," said Marilee.

"Thank you for asking, Marilee," said Zeke.

"I appreciate your offer. But Cassie is going to be my partner."

Cassie loved the stunned look that crossed the other girl's face. Marilee Tischler was used to getting everything she wanted. Well, she couldn't have Zeke.

Just then a murmur ran through the crowd. Cassie looked up to see Ben approaching. "Careful, Zeke," she whispered.

"I just want to speak with him," said Zeke.

Ben passed through the throng of kids waiting eagerly to see what would happen. When he reached the center of the circle, he stopped and faced Zeke.

The alien moved toward Ben cautiously, his hands hanging loosely at his sides. He stopped before he reached the bully.

"I do not want to fight you, Ben," he said.

"I knew you were chicken!" the other boy snarled.

"There is no reason for us to be enemies," Zeke said calmly. "If you are angry that I beat you in the arcade, perhaps you would like a rematch."

Ben clenched his fists.

Zeke took a step back.

Ben lunged at Zeke.

Zeke jumped out of the way.

Ben swung.

Zeke ducked.

Ben swung again.

Zeke slipped under his arm.

"Fight!" cried someone from the crowd.

"Come on, Zeke. You can do it!" Marilee called. Cassie glared at her. She didn't want Zeke to get hurt. But even worse, she thought, was the possibility that Zeke would do something to draw attention to his being an alien.

That was when Cassie saw him—the man at the edge of the crowd, the man with the wire-rimmed glasses, the one man who might just know about Zeke.

Grant Trexler.

Cassie had first seen Grant Trexler on a school trip to the National Weather Bureau, where he worked as an astronomer. Bored with a lecture on weather patterns, Cassie had decided to do some spying around the bureau. She had overheard Grant talking about aliens. Convinced that a spaceship had recently landed in Hillsdale, he was obsessed with capturing the travelers.

Unfortunately, Grant had caught Cassie spying. With Zeke's help, she had escaped him. But now Grant just kept showing up. She had seen him in the field near the spaceship and lingering outside her house. Now here he was in their school yard. What was he doing here?

14

Had he seen the ship land the second time? Did he have any proof that Zeke was an alien? All Cassie knew for sure was that she had to get Zeke away—and fast.

Just then, a cry rose up from the crowd. Cassie turned her head in time to see Ben lunging at Zeke. Zeke staggered but recovered his balance. Cassie saw his hands go rigid. This time when Ben rushed at him Zeke dodged him and landed a solid karate chop on the bully's shoulder.

Ben fell to the ground.

The crowd cheered.

Cassie looked over at Grant Trexler. Their eyes met, and he saluted. Cassie gasped, then moved past the circle of children and grabbed Zeke's hand.

"Let's get out of here," she whispered.

"Why?" asked Zeke, watching as two boys helped Ben to his feet.

"He's here!" said Cassie.

"Who's here?" asked Zeke.

"That Trexler guy from the weather bureau. The one who followed me to the ship. He's right over there!"

Cassie turned to point at Grant. But the man from the weather bureau was gone.

CHAPTER

3

"Zeke, trust me," said Cassie. "We've got to get out of here fast."

She pulled the alien past the crowd of students eager to congratulate him. When they reached the outer edge of the school yard, Cassie and Zeke broke into a run. They didn't stop until they were half a mile away. Finally Cassie collapsed at the base of a tree on a street corner. Zeke sat down beside her.

"How come you're not out of breath?" Cassie gasped.

Zeke shrugged, his eyes scanning the street for any sign of the astronomer.

"We lost him!" Cassie said, still panting a bit.

The alien was silent. Cassie sensed that something was wrong. "Zeke, is something the matter?" she asked.

"I do not like to fight," Zeke said simply.

"Maybe not," laughed Cassie. "But you're great at it!"

"It is not funny, Cassie," said Zeke. "I could have hurt him. My skills are far beyond his."

"Well, you didn't hurt him," said Cassie. "Okay, you hurt his pride. But other than that, he was fine. By the way, where did you learn karate?"

"Karate?" said Zeke. "What is karate?"

"What do you call that chop you gave to Ben's shoulder?"

"That is one of the Coranian fighting techniques. I mastered those at the Earth age of seven," Zeke explained.

"And I suppose that's normal for all Triminicans?" asked Cassie.

"Of course," said Zeke.

"Well, if anyone asks you what it was, say you studied karate. Okay?"

Zeke shrugged. "Okay. If you say so."

Just then a car stopped across the street. Cassie gasped as she saw Grant Trexler getting out of it.

Zeke saw him, too. Without a word, the two friends leapt to their feet and began running again, darting over perfectly green lawns and doubling back between hedges. Cassie followed close on the alien's heels but could still hear Grant Trexler's heavy breathing behind her.

"Faster!" she screamed.

Zeke turned as he ran. When he saw how close the astronomer was, he picked up his pace. Cassie could barely keep up with him. Her only hope was that Trexler was in worse shape than she was. Come on, feet, she thought. Run!

They flew down one street and up another, around corners and over lawns. Finally, Zeke made a sharp turn into an overgrown backyard. Cassie followed a moment later—and quickly screeched to a halt. Zeke was standing still, staring up at a fence that was at least ten feet high. There was no way out.

"Hurry up," gasped Cassie. "Climb!"

"I have a better idea," said Zeke, fumbling in his pocket. He pulled out a flat golden object that looked like a hardened pancake. Zeke punched at the row of flickering buttons on it.

"Ready?" he asked Cassie, taking her hand.

"Ready!" Cassie exclaimed.

Zeke threw the disk. It arced high and wide, then boomeranged back. At the exact moment it would have hit Zeke, the disk spun out and began circling the two friends. Grant Trexler rounded the corner just in time to watch them disappear in a circle of sparkling light.

Less then ten seconds later, Cassie and Zeke appeared in the main room of the spaceship. Spot was there to greet them.

"You were forbidden to use the materializer," he droned.

"And how was your day, Spot?" asked Cassie, sitting down. Her legs were shaking. She wasn't sure if it was from all the running or from fear.

"You were forbidden to use the materializer," the robot repeated.

Zeke sighed. "It was necessary. We were being followed."

"By whom?" asked Spot, moving toward the window of the ship and gazing out into the field.

Zeke ignored his question. "Is the invisibility shield activated?" he asked the robot.

"Of course," said Spot.

"I guess we're safe then," said Cassie, breathing a sigh of relief. "At least for now." She got up on shaking legs and moved toward the refrigerator. Zeke stretched and took off his wig. He often did this on the ship, saying his head got hot after a while.

"Hey, Spot," said Cassie as she searched for something familiar to drink. "Do you want to help Zeke and me come up with a science project for school?"

"Why don't you build a robot?" asked Spot.

Cassie laughed.

"Zeke, I swear Spot is developing a sense of humor," she said, carrying two glasses and a pitcher of orange liquid to the table.

"What is so funny about building a robot?" asked Spot.

"Nothing at all," said Cassie. "Why don't we just bring you to the science fair?"

"An excellent idea," said Spot.

"Forget it," said Zeke.

Cassie sipped her drink. Like every other liquid on the ship, it tasted like melted Jell-O. She stared at Spot and thought about the science competition. They would definitely win with a robot. But it would also draw too much attention to Zeke. And what if Grant Trexler were still lurking about?

Grant! He was getting too close for comfort.

"We must do something about the astronomer," said Zeke, as if reading Cassie's thoughts.

"I know," said Cassie. "He's really becoming a problem. You don't think there's any chance he followed us here, do you?"

"I don't see how he could have," said Zeke. "But just to be sure—Robot, watch out the window of the ship for a while and report any movements you see."

Spot moved obediently to the window.

"So," said Zeke, "tell me about this science competition."

Cassie opened her mouth to speak. But the robot called out first.

"Humanoid in the field!"

Zeke and Cassie leapt up from the table in a single movement, racing for the window. In the field below, a figure dressed in a hat and trench coat stood peering down at a device in his hand. They couldn't see his face, but it was obvious that he was searching for something.

"Grant!" Cassie exclaimed.

"I wonder how he followed us?" said Zeke.

"I don't think he did," said Cassie. "Before you tried to return to your planet the last time, he was already nosing around this field, remember? He must have just come back here on his own."

"Spot, report on the device in his hand," said Zeke.

"Device known as magnetic field variable detector," said the robot. "Used for discerning magnetic fields."

"Oh no," said Cassie. "Can he detect the invisibility shield?"

"Not exactly," said Zeke. "The shield is composed of trans-configured hydroxyls. But a magnetic field does surround the ship."

21

"At least he can't see us," said Cassie. "He can't, can he?"

"No, of course not," said Zeke.

They watched the man examining, exploring, searching the area around the ship.

"A blast from the laser banks would disintegrate the humanoid in one point three seconds," Spot reported.

"What?" gasped Cassie.

"NO!" Zeke cried. "He still has no proof that we are here. Do nothing."

"I wonder what Grant Trexler is doing with a . . . a . . . what is it called again?" asked Cassie.

"A magnetic field variable detector," Spot repeated.

"And when did he have time to change his clothes?" Cassie wondered.

Just then the man looked up.

Cassie and Zeke gasped.

It wasn't Grant Trexler. This man had a huge, fleshy face, with dark bushy eyebrows and a snarl etched into his features. And he was staring into the window. Right at Cassie and Zeke!

CHAPTER

The two friends froze. They knew the man couldn't actually see them. But something about the way he was staring right into the window of the spaceship sent a chill down Cassie's spine.

"Who is he?" she whispered.

"Perhaps the astronomer sent him," said Zeke.

"What should we do?"

"Determine the frequency of the detector and send the humanoid searching elsewhere," droned Spot.

"Really?" asked Cassie. "Can we do that?"

"In order to accomplish this, we must have the device in our possession," said the robot.

"Oh, great, I'll just go out there and ask him for it." Cassie spoke sarcastically, though her heart was pounding in her ears.

The man began circling the ship.

"Robot, can we deactivate the device?" asked Zeke.

"Negative," said the robot. "Not without knowledge of the transmitting frequency."

"Zeke, we're spies. We should do something!" said Cassie.

"You are correct," said Zeke. "We must lure him away from the ship."

Zeke paced the floor of the spaceship, deep in thought, while Cassie and Spot kept an eye on the man in the trench coat.

He thought for a moment. "I've got it!" he said. "We shall materialize outside the ship and then run away from it. The man will follow."

"Yeah, but what if he catches us?" asked Cassie.

Suddenly the robot spoke up. "Another humanoid approaching at four degrees mark zero."

Cassie and Zeke raced back to the window. "Where?" asked Cassie. "I don't see anyone."

"He will be within viewing range in two minutes," Spot reported.

"He?" asked Cassie.

"The humanoid is male," droned the robot.

Zeke and Cassie looked at each other, then spoke at the same time. "Grant!"

Sure enough, in precisely two minutes, the

familiar figure of Grant Trexler came into view, striding across the field.

"He must be having a rendezvous with the man in the trench coat," said Cassie.

"Shall I eliminate him?" asked Spot.

Cassie turned to face Spot, her hands on her hips. "For your information, we do not go around eliminating people on Earth."

"We don't do it on Triminica, either," said Zeke. "Robot, what has gotten into you?"

"I have been learning Earth customs," said Spot.

"Well, you're learning them incorrectly," said Cassie. Then, suddenly, she burst out laughing. "Spot, have you figured out a way to watch television?"

"Affirmative," said Spot. "I am particularly fond of the monochrome programs with John Wayne and the very colorful termination programs with the Schwarzenegger humanoid."

"Who?" asked Zeke.

Cassie grinned at her friend. "I'll explain later."

The three of them turned back to the window. Grant had stopped in the middle of the field. He looked around and seemed confused.

"He knows we are here," said Zeke. "He just does not know where."

25

"He will when he meets up with his friend," said Cassie. "Besides, Zeke, the invisibility shield is great and all that, but what if one of them bumps into the ship?"

"You are right, Cassie. We must prevent that," said Zeke. He turned toward Spot. "Robot, do we have any fuel left?"

"There is a small fuel supply remaining," droned Spot.

"I don't understand," said Cassie. "I thought it was all used up."

Zeke grinned at her. "We do not have enough to leave the Earth's orbit. But there is something we can do to prevent these nosy men from, as you say, 'bumping into' the ship."

He moved swiftly toward the center of the control panel. "Robot, assist!"

"Elevation level?" asked the robot.

"Fifty feet," Zeke said.

Cassie watched in confusion while the Triminican and his robot activated the ship's computer. A soft humming sound rose from the transparent cylinder in the center of the room, and slowly the pink liquid inside it began to bubble.

Suddenly Cassie felt lightheaded. "What happened?" she asked.

"Look," said Zeke, pointing out the window.

Cassie peered out and gasped. She was looking down at the ground from fifty feet up in the air.

"Zeke, that's brilliant!" Cassie exclaimed. "No one will bump into the ship now."

"I know," said Zeke, grinning.

"How long can we stay up here?" asked Cassie.

"Until the fuel runs out," said Zeke. "At this elevation, fuel consumption is minimal. We could remain here for several hours. But for obvious reasons, we will descend as soon as they leave."

Cassie, Zeke, and Spot looked out the window at the ground below. They watched the man in the trench coat snooping around the ship. They watched Grant scoping out the field.

Then an amazing thing happened. The man in the trench coat saw Grant. For a moment, he stopped moving completely. Then, suddenly, he dove for the dense thicket of trees that surrounded the ship.

"He's hiding!" said Cassie. "I don't get it."

For almost half an hour, they watched as Grant Trexler explored the field and the area surrounding it. But he didn't find the ship, and he didn't find the man in the trench coat. As the sun began its descent in the sky, Grant finally gave up his search and left the field.

That was when the man in the trench coat began following him.

As Spot brought the ship back down to earth, Zeke slipped on his wig, and he and Cassie put on their spy belts. Ignoring Spot's protests, the two spies then slipped out and followed the man in the trench coat.

They kept their distance, dodging behind trees and cars so that the man in the trench coat would not see them. A hundred feet ahead, Grant Trexler walked slowly. He seemed to have no idea he was being followed. The man in the trench coat, however, was suspicious. He kept looking over his shoulder in Cassie and Zeke's direction.

"He seems awfully smart," Cassie whispered to Zeke. "Smarter than the Trexler guy. Maybe he's a real spy."

"Maybe he is," grinned Zeke. "But he's no match for a spy from the Interstellar Spy Academy."

"I hope you're right," said Cassie as the man turned again and they ducked behind a row of garbage cans.

Grant Trexler lived in a small house in a row of other small houses across from a small park in the center of Hillsdale. He moved swiftly through the streets of the town, never looking behind him, never noticing the trail of spies in his wake.

When he reached his house he disappeared inside, the front door swinging shut behind him.

Cassie and Zeke watched from the park while the man in the trench coat studied the house. Activating the device in his hand, he scanned the house for a magnetic field. But when the device registered nothing, he turned and walked away.

"We should follow him," said Zeke.

"Absolutely," said Cassie. But as they left the park, she noticed the setting sun. She looked at her watch and groaned. "Zeke, I have to get home for dinner."

"Then I will follow him," Zeke decided quickly. "You stay here and make sure Trexler does not leave the house—at least until I am gone. Then go home. We will use our walkie-talkies to communicate."

"I could stay longer if I had a materializer disk to go home with," Cassie said hopefully.

Zeke grinned and reached into his pocket. He handed Cassie one of the golden pancakes. "Do you remember the coordinates for your house?"

"Yep," said Cassie. She glanced down the street. The man in the trench coat was getting away. "You'd better hurry, Zeke," she said, plucking the walkie-talkie from her spy belt.

Her alien friend raced after the man. "Be careful," she added softly.

CHAPTER

When Cassie opened her eyes the next morning, the first thing she saw was another pair of eyes. Eye sockets, actually. Huge, hollow eye sockets, peering down at her. She was suddenly wide awake.

"Spot," she whispered. "What are you doing here?"

"Where is Zekephlon?" asked the robot, calling Zeke by his full Triminican name.

"I don't know." Cassie rubbed her eyes and sat up. "Didn't he return to the ship last night?"

"Negative," responded the robot.

"Okay, don't panic," said Cassie, trying not to panic herself. "I'll just get dressed and we'll look for him. Turn around."

"Why?"

"Because I'm in my pajamas. Turn around so I can get up and get dressed."

"If you are permitted to view me covered in this absurd keratin growth you call hair, why can I not view you in your pajamas?" asked Spot.

Cassie had to admit that it was a good question. And besides, she reminded herself, he *is* a robot. But still . . .

There was a knock at the door, and Cassie's younger brother called out, "Cass? You up?"

"Just a second, Simon," Cassie called back, springing out of bed.

"Get in the closet," she said to Spot.

"Why?"

"Just do it," said Cassie, pushing the robot in among the tangle of clothes and shoes on her closet floor. "And be quiet!"

Closing the closet door, she called for her brother to come in. A five-year-old boy entered, smiling.

"Who were you talking to, Cass?" he asked.

"No one," said Cassie.

"Sure you were. I heard you," said Simon.

Cassie sighed. "Simon, did anyone ever tell you that you're entirely too perceptive for a five-year-old?"

"Sure," said Simon. "What's perceptive?"

Cassie laughed.

From across the room, the walkie-talkie on her spy belt crackled.

"Wow! What's that?" asked Simon, running over and peering down at it.

"Cassie, come in," Zeke's voice called through the walkie-talkie.

"WOW!" the little boy cried. "Someone's trying to contact you!"

Cassie half expected Spot to come bursting out of the closet.

She put her hands gently on Simon's shoulders and pointed him toward the bedroom door.

"It's just a friend at school," said Cassie. "He has the other walkie-talkie."

"Can I talk to him?"

"No," said Cassie. "Go downstairs. I have to get dressed."

"Cassie!" Zeke's voice crackled again.

"Answer it!" commanded Spot from the closet.

"Who's that?" asked Simon, whirling around. Cassie tried to stop her brother, but the small boy ducked under her arms and lunged for the closet door. His chubby hand turned the knob and pulled the door open.

Then he screamed.

Cassie flew to Simon's side, grabbed him, and put her hand over his mouth. The small boy wriggled to get free. But Cassie kept her hand in place, talking calmly. "It's okay, Simon.

It's okay. I'll let you go. Just promise you won't scream again."

The boy wriggled wildly but nodded his head. Cassie let him go.

Simon stared at Spot. The robot stared back. They were the same size.

"Wow!" said Simon softly.

"Wow, yourself," said Spot.

"What are you?" asked Simon.

"What are *you*?" asked Spot.

What am I going to do? thought Cassie.

The walkie-talkie crackled again. Cassie crossed the room and picked it up. "Don't say anything, Zeke. I'll meet you at the school yard in fifteen minutes. Over and out."

"Right," said Zeke. "Over and out."

"Cassie?" said Mr. Williams from outside her bedroom door. "Is everything all right? Did I hear a scream?"

"Don't come in, Dad. I'm getting dressed."

"Is your brother with you?"

"Uh . . . yeah. He walked in on me while I was dressing. I pushed him in the closet. That's why he screamed." It was sort of the truth.

"Let him out this instant," demanded Mr. Williams.

Cassie opened the door a crack, pushed her brother out, and closed the door. Then she held her breath. She knew what was coming.

"Dad, there's a robot in Cassie's closet and people talking to her on the walkie-talkie," Simon's voice faded as he followed their father down the stairs.

"That's nice, son," said Mr. Williams. "What would you like for breakfast?"

Cassie breathed a sigh of relief. Fortunately, her parents were used to Simon's overactive imagination. They had heard this kind of story before. She opened the closet door again.

"Spot, you've got to leave now. It's too dangerous."

"Negative," said the robot. "I will accompany you to your meeting with Zeke. I must determine whether he is safe."

"No."

"Yes."

"No."

Cassie sighed. She really didn't have a choice. There was no way of forcing the robot to leave. She went downstairs long enough to grab two doughnuts and tell her parents she had to meet a friend before school to talk about their science project. Then she raced back upstairs.

"With the safety of Zekephlon in question, I have determined that use of a materializer disk is warranted," said Spot.

"Fine," said Cassie. "But we're not going anywhere until we fix your wigs and you get down on all fours like a good dog."

Spot mumbled and grumbled as Cassie adjusted the wigs on his body. She stood back and admired her work.

"Now walk like a dog!" she demanded.

"Your television viewing programs have robots in them. I fail to see why— "

"Just do what I say!" Cassie interrupted.

Moments later, Cassie and Spot materialized in the school yard. Zeke was waiting for them.

Hidden from view, Grant Trexler waited, too.

CHAPTER 6

"There you are, Robot!" exclaimed Zeke.

"And there *you* are," said Spot.

"I returned to the ship this morning and you were gone," said Zeke. "I thought I gave you specific orders not to leave the ship."

"When you did not return, I went in search of you," Spot explained. "It is consistent with my programming."

"He went searching for you in *my* bedroom," said Cassie.

"I encountered a small Earth boy," said Spot.

"WHAT? Cassie, what happened?"

"Nothing. He just met Simon," said Cassie. She glanced around the school yard and shivered. "I've never been here this early before. It's kind of creepy when it's empty."

"I do not know about creepy," said Zeke. "But I think I am being followed."

"By whom?" asked Cassie.

Zeke shrugged. "One of our friends, I guess," he said.

"But which one?" asked Cassie, looking over her shoulder nervously.

"Probably Trexler," said Zeke. "I left our friend in the trench coat at the Hillsdale Arms Hotel."

"Is that where you were all night?" demanded the robot.

Zeke nodded. "I followed him there and stayed in the lobby all night. He never left his room. Number 316, in case you are interested."

"Look, Zeke, if someone *is* following you, Spot had better get lost," said Cassie.

"Of course. Robot, return to the ship at once!" Zeke ordered.

"Not without you," said Spot.

"I must attend school today. You *will* return to the ship at once."

"Unless you want to risk being caught by the dogcatcher again," said Cassie.

The robot rose quickly onto two feet. "I will not be mistaken for a dog again!"

"Spot—down!" Cassie cried.

"No!" said Spot.

"This is ridiculous," said Cassie. "Would you prefer to be caught by the dogcatcher or by almost anyone looking at you now?"

"Explain," said Spot.

"On all fours you look like a freaked-out dog of some sort. Standing like this, talking to us, you look like some kind of robot covered in wigs."

"Which is precisely what I am!" stated Spot.

"Well, well," snarled a voice behind Cassie. "What have we here?"

Cassie whirled and found herself face-to-face with Grant Trexler.

"Wha-what are you doing here?" Cassie stammered.

"The question is, what is *he* doing here?" Grant growled, pointing at Zeke. Then he pointed at Spot. "And what is *that* doing here?"

"I am here to attend school," said Zeke, without batting an eye.

"Do you always travel to another planet to go to school?" asked Grant, smirking.

"No," said Zeke. "Usually I inhabit the body of some unsuspecting Earthling."

"Very funny, kid," snarled Grant. Then he leaned forward and spoke menacingly, his mouth only an inch from Zeke's face.

"I just wanted to let you in on a secret," he said, poking a finger into Zeke's chest. "I know you're an alien"—*poke, poke*—"I know this stu-

pid-looking dog of yours isn't a dog"—*poke,
poke*—"And I know that somewhere"—*poke*—
"in that field"—*poke*—"you've got a spaceship"—*poke, poke.*

The poking was a huge mistake on Grant's
part. Spot thought he was physically threatening Zeke. In a flash, the robot grabbed the astronomer, wrapped his hairy metal arms
around Grant, and hoisted the man above his
head. Grant struggled and screamed.

"Let me down, you beast!"

"He thought you were attacking me," said
Zeke simply.

"I said, let me down, you hairy monster!"

"Let him down," said Zeke.

Spot put the astronomer down. Immediately
Grant leapt to his feet, whirled around, and—
in a moment of incredible stupidity—swung at
Spot with his arm. There was a sound of bone
meeting metal. Grant cried out and grabbed his
arm.

"You broke my arm, you mutant!" he bel-
lowed.

"If I were you, I wouldn't call him any more
names," said Cassie.

Grant sank to the ground with a moan, his
arm dangling limply at his side.

"Is it really broken?" Cassie asked. She suddenly felt kind of sorry for Grant.

"What do you think, kid?" snarled the astronomer.

"I think that you should go to a hospital and have your arm checked out," said Cassie. She turned to Zeke, her eyes twinkling. "What do you think, Zeke?"

"I think that is an excellent idea," said Zeke, picking up on Cassie's meaning. With the robot's help, Zeke punched the necessary information into the computer. Then he pointed to the moaning scientist. "Move away from him."

Cassie moved.

"What are you doing, alien?" Grant said, his voice shaking. He took a step toward Zeke, who moved back swiftly.

Grant lunged for the Triminican.

Zeke threw the disk and ducked.

The disk circled Grant. Faster and faster, the sparkling lights spiraled around the astronomer.

"What the . . . ?" shrieked Grant, trying to grab with his good arm at the wisps of light that encircled him.

And then, suddenly, in a flash of light, Grant Trexler was gone!

Cassie looked at Zeke and grinned. "Did you send him to the hospital?" she asked.

"Absolutely," said Zeke, grinning back.

"Good!" said Cassie. "Now I can stop worrying about his arm and go back to hating him."

At that moment, a car pulled into the parking lot of the school. The first teacher had arrived. The school yard would soon be flooded with children.

"Spot, you *must* leave now," Cassie told the robot. Spot had not moved or said a word since Trexler hit him.

"Affirmative," said the robot.

"Let me send you back by materializer," said Zeke.

"You will return to the ship immediately following your last class?" asked the robot.

"I promise," said Zeke.

Cassie waited while Zeke and Spot ducked behind the school building. By the time Zeke reappeared, buses were arriving at the school. It was only seven-thirty in the morning, but Cassie was exhausted and scared. The astronomer had gone from being an inconvenience to being a major problem. And just because Zeke had sent him away this time didn't mean he was gone for good. And what about the man in the trench coat? Who was he? Why was he staying in the hotel? Cassie took a deep breath and steadied herself. At least Zeke had taken care of Ben the bully. As Cassie saw it, that made school the least aggravating place to be.

Cassie was wrong. Science, the second class of the day, presented yet another problem.

"I have an announcement," said Ms. Grayson. "This year, the science fair will no longer be an optional contest."

A groan rose from the children in the class.

"However," Ms. Grayson continued, "there will not be a midterm test either."

The groans turned to cheers.

"Settle down," said Ms. Grayson. "As I was saying, the science fair will serve as your midterm. As always, you must enter in girl-boy teams. This year, the teams have been chosen for you. I have posted a list on the bulletin board. Please consult it at the end of class."

The teacher gestured at a stack of papers on the edge of her desk. "These are the rules for the fair. It is no longer a contest. You will be graded on three things: how well you follow the rules, the originality of your project, and its success. Now, let's open our books to page twenty-one."

Cassie didn't hear one word Ms. Grayson said after "the teams have been chosen for you." A wave of panic washed over her, and she spent the rest of the class staring at the paper tacked to the bulletin board. When the bell rang, Cassie flew across the room. Her heart dove into her stomach when she saw her name:

CASSIE WILLIAMS/BEN O'BRIEN

And right beneath it:

ZEKE WILLIAMS/MARILEE TISCHLER

At exactly nine-thirty that night, Cassie material-ized in the main room of the spaceship. She was dressed all in black, except for her coat. She had put on the green-and-red parka as an afterthought. It would hide her spy belt and keep her warm.

Zeke was waiting. "Any problems?" he asked.

"None," said Cassie. "My parents think I went to bed early."

"Is that it?" Zeke motioned at the shopping bag in Cassie's hand.

"It sure is!" said Cassie. "The stuff was in our attic, just like I thought."

Zeke and Cassie had decided Spot needed a new disguise. Dogs might not be allowed in the hotel. The robot hated the idea but said that he didn't think anything could be worse than looking like a dog.

Zeke and Cassie removed the wigs from Spot with a Triminican glue dissolver. Then they dressed him in the new disguise and stood back to admire their work.

"This is humiliating," mumbled Spot. Cassie grinned. The robot was becoming more human every day.

"You look great, Spot," she said. "Or should I say Miss Spot." She giggled.

The robot was wearing a dress. A frilly, little girl dress with a white collar and cuffs. Cassie hadn't worn it in years.

"Sorry about the shoes," she said.

"Why are you sorrier about the shoes than about the dress?" said Spot.

"They clash," Cassie giggled, staring at the worn, clunky brown shoes that she had squeezed the robot's feet into. "But they were the only ones I could find. Oh," she said. "I almost forgot." She pulled a purse out of the shopping bag and handed it to Spot.

"What is this for?" asked the robot.

"Just carry it!" said Cassie. "It matches the dress."

Spot grumbled and mumbled, but slipped the purse over his arm.

Zeke smiled at the robot. "At least you get to walk on two feet now," he said.

Spot muttered something under his breath.

"Are we ready?" asked Zeke.

"Ready!" said Cassie. "Let's go break into old Bushy Eyes's room."

Zeke chuckled. "Bushy Eyes!" he said. "I like it. An appropriate name for him, Cassie."

They materialized outside the hotel at nine-forty-five. Zeke and Spot followed Cassie into the hotel and straight to the house phone. Cassie called room 316. There was no answer. The man in the trench coat was not in his room.

Spot got one or two stares from the other people in the lobby, but no one stopped them as they boarded the elevator to the third floor.

Zeke pulled out a vial and filled a small ray gun with liquid zorcanian 6, a Triminican metal dissolver.

"Is the coast clear?" Zeke whispered.

Cassie glanced up and down the hallway.

"Check!" she said.

Zeke aimed the gun at the doorknob of room 316 and pressed the trigger. A stream of amber-colored liquid shot out of the gun. The metal doorknob dissolved, dripping down the door.

The three spies slipped inside. "Cassie, guard the door," said Zeke.

Cassie took a position at the entrance to the room.

The magnetic field variable detector was sitting on the nightstand. Spot saw it instantly and moved swiftly toward the device.

That was when Cassie heard the running water coming from the bathroom.

"Zeke!" she whispered loudly across the room. But the Triminican was examining the field detector with Spot.

"Zeke!" Cassie called, louder this time.

Zeke looked up.

"He's in there!" Cassie mouthed, frantically pointing to the bathroom door.

Zeke's head swiveled in the direction Cassie was pointing. He heard the running water and the color drained from his face.

Then, suddenly, both Cassie and Zeke heard something worse than running water. They heard nothing. The man was out of the shower!

The phone rang.

The doorknob on the bathroom door turned.

In a flash, Zeke pushed Spot into the only closet in the room and stepped in after him. Cassie slipped into the hallway.

Bushy Eyes stepped out of the bathroom, a towel around his waist. Looking suspiciously around him, he picked up the phone.

CHAPTER

Cassie was standing outside Bushy Eyes's room, searching in her spy belt for the listening device, when she heard a voice behind her.

"Is there a problem, Miss?"

She whirled around and found herself facing a boy of about twenty. He was wearing a porter's uniform on his body and a peculiar look on his face.

"Uh, no problem," said Cassie, moving so she stood directly in front of the melted lock. "I'm just looking for my key."

"To which room?"

"To my room, of course," Cassie snapped nervously.

The porter looked at the number on the door.

"But this is Mr. Kolnikov's room," he said. "Perhaps you'd better show me your key."

"I just told you I can't find it!" Cassie snapped again. The more nervous she became, the snippier her voice was getting.

"Well, why don't we go down to the front desk and get you another one?" said the porter. He reached for Cassie's arm, but she stepped back before he could touch her.

"Uh, I just remembered I'm on the wrong floor," said Cassie. "Thanks anyway."

She tried to move past the porter, but he blocked her way.

"Are you sure you're a guest here?" he asked. "This is a pretty small hotel, and I don't remember seeing you here before."

"I . . . uh . . . just checked in," said Cassie.

"Hey—what happened to that lock?" said the porter.

Cassie moved to block his view again, her brain working furiously to come up with an answer. Suddenly there was a brilliant flash of light behind the porter, and Zeke and Spot materialized in the hallway. In one expert motion, Zeke laid a perfectly executed karate chop to the porter's neck. The porter dropped to the ground and lay motionless.

"What did you do that for?" Cassie whispered. "I would have gotten away."

"There is no time for discussion, Cassie," said Zeke. "We must listen now."

Cassie knew Zeke was right. There was no time to lose. She located the listening device in her spy belt, slipped on the earphones, and attached the metal bug to the door.

"This is outrageous!" snarled a heavily accented voice in her ear. "I must have more money now or I will not continue. . . ."

There was silence as the man listened to a response on the phone. Then the man began shouting.

"How dare you treat me this way! I was an agent for the greatest spy organization in the world. I will find out who you are. I will track you down. I will . . ."

Silence again.

And then, "As I told you, I am close on their trail. . . . Yes, yes, there are definitely extraterrestrials here. Now, will you meet my terms or not?"

There was a long, long silence. Cassie glanced nervously at the still body of the porter. If he woke and saw Spot or remembered to check the melted lock . . .

The man was speaking again. "Very well. Deposit the money in my account tomorrow morning. I will not proceed until the check has cleared."

The man hung up the phone.

The porter groaned.

"Let's get out of here!" said Cassie.

Zeke pulled a materializer disk out of his pocket and set the coordinates. The porter raised his head just as Cassie, Zeke, and Spot disappeared in a cloud of twinkling light. He groaned and held his head.

Cassie slid back into bed at midnight. She slept restlessly, dreaming of spies and spaceships and out-of-this-world science experiments. In the morning she was so tired she couldn't make herself get out of bed—until her mother came in to tell her she was late for school. After sliding into the same clothes she had worn the day before, Cassie ran toward school. She heard the second bell ring long before she reached the building and slowed down to a walk. She was already late. She was already in trouble. Five more minutes wouldn't make a difference one way or the other.

Cassie saw Grant Trexler as soon as she reached the steps leading up to the school. He was standing beneath a tree, wearing the same wire-rimmed glasses and overcoat that Cassie had come to know so well. But there was something different about him. It wasn't until after Cassie had ignored his call and raced past him into the school that she figured out what that difference was. Grant Trexler was wearing a plaster cast. He really had broken his arm.

When Cassie walked into her first class, Mr. Harrison, the social studies teacher, stopped talking and glared at her.

"You're late!" he said.

"No kidding!" Cassie snipped.

A low rumble of laughter echoed through the classroom. Mr. Harrison turned a light shade of red. Cassie looked at him apologetically but said nothing.

The teacher sighed. "Take your seat," he said. Then he turned his back to the class and continued the lecture while he drew Thomas Jefferson's family tree on the blackboard.

Cassie opened her notebook and scribbled a note to Zeke.

"Trexler outside. Arm in cast."

She folded the note until it was small enough to fit into the palm of her hand and passed it to Zeke, who sat next to her. Zeke read the note, smiled, and wrote a reply.

"Robot and I have a plan. What is a cast?" Cassie read when she got the note back. She looked over at Zeke and mouthed, "What's the plan?"

Zeke ripped a small piece of paper from his notebook, scribbled another reply, and passed it to Cassie. But before Cassie could unfold the note, a shadow passed over her desk. She looked up into the stern face of Mr. Harrison.

"I'll take that, Miss Williams," said the teacher.

Cassie panicked. She could think of only one thing to do. In a single fluid motion, with the eyes of the entire class on her, Cassie stuffed the small piece of paper into her mouth, chewed a few times, and swallowed.

The class shrieked its approval.

Cassie looked up at Mr. Harrison, smiled, and shrugged.

"The principal's office!" roared the teacher. "Both of you! Now!"

CHAPTER

Principal Levine stared at the two students and shook his head. Cassie kept wiping at her mouth with her hand and swallowing. Her tongue was pasty, and there was a lump in her throat she couldn't get rid of. She didn't understand why spies in the movies swallowed secret notes. They tasted disgusting.

"Frankly, I'm disappointed," said the principal.

"It won't happen again," said Cassie. She swallowed hard. It wasn't a lie. There was no way she would eat paper again.

The principal consulted a file folder on his desk.

"Cassie, since your cousin arrived in Hillsdale two weeks ago, you have been late to school three times, your grades are falling, and you seem to have developed a behavioral problem. I'm afraid I'm going to have to call your parents."

"Oh, please don't do that," Cassie begged. "I promise it won't happen again."

"What won't happen again?"

"All of it. Everything you just said," said Cassie. She smiled what she considered to be her most charming smile.

It didn't work. The principal frowned and turned his attention to Zeke. "When exactly will your parents be arriving in Hillsdale?" he asked.

Zeke glanced at Cassie.

"Next week," she said.

"I'm speaking to Zeke," said Principal Levine.

"Next week," said Zeke.

The principal sighed. "That's what you said last week."

"They've been held up," said Cassie. "But they'll be here soon."

"Do you always answer for your cousin?"

"We're very close," said Cassie.

The principal looked to the heavens and sighed again. "This is your last warning," he said sternly. "If either of you is sent to this office again, I will contact Cassie's parents. Is that clear?"

"Absolutely," said Cassie, rising from her seat.

"I'm not finished," said the principal. Cassie sat down again.

"Zeke, how are you getting along?" the principal asked.

"Fine," said Zeke.

"No problems with the other students?"

"No. None," said Zeke.

"How about Ben O'Brien?"

Cassie groaned softly. Even the principal had heard about the fight. Suddenly she had an idea.

"Ben is so mad about the fight that he's threatening me now, too," she said. "And Ms. Grayson wants me to be partners with him for the science experiment. Maybe you could arrange it so Zeke and I could be partners?"

The principal leveled his eyes at Cassie.

"Miss Williams, you know that I do not interfere with classroom business. If Ms. Grayson teamed you with Ben, I'm sure she had a reason."

"But—"

"That is all. You may go now."

Cassie and Zeke rose to leave. As they reached the door, Principal Levine called after them. "And the minute your parents get into town, I want to meet them, Zeke."

"Great," whispered Cassie. "Another problem. Just what we need."

Sending Zeke and Cassie to the principal's

office wasn't enough for Mr. Harrison. He made them stay after school and wash Jefferson's family tree off the blackboard and then straighten up all the books in the room. By the time they left the school, Grant Trexler was no longer outside. But that didn't mean he was gone for good, and both Cassie and Zeke knew it. Grant would be back. And Mr. Kolnikov, if that was really his name, would be back, too.

"At least old Bushy Eyes will leave us alone until he gets his money from whomever he was talking to," said Cassie as they walked to the ship. Zeke had been as tired as Cassie that morning and had forgotten to bring an extra materializer disk.

"When he returns, we will be ready for him," said Zeke.

"I almost forgot!" said Cassie. "What's the plan you and Spot came up with?"

Zeke grinned. "It is a great plan, Cassie. You are going to love it."

"Tell me!"

"Actually, Spot came up with the idea. . . ." Zeke let his voice trail off.

"Come on, tell me!" cried Cassie, jumping in front of Zeke so he had to stop walking.

"Okay, okay." Zeke laughed. "But move out of the way. We have to get back to the ship."

Cassie moved. "Well?" she asked.

"We have the frequency for the magnetic field variable detector," Zeke explained.

"I know," said Cassie. "Spot got it in the hotel room just before the phone rang."

"Right," said Zeke. "Last night, Spot suggested that we beat the grass to lure the tiger from the mountain."

"What? What does that mean?" cried Cassie.

"You do not have that expression?" asked Zeke.

"I don't think so," said Cassie.

"It means that to make the man go away, we need to lure him to another destination," Zeke explained.

"And?"

"And . . . we thought we would send him to Trexler's house!"

Cassie stopped dead in her tracks. "Zeke," she said, her voice barely a whisper, "that's brilliant!"

"I know," said Zeke.

"Maybe he'll think that Trexler's the alien!"

"That is the idea," said Zeke.

"But how?"

"We will plant things in Trexler's house, maybe change his appearance. We have not yet worked out all the details. Come on, Cassie— we have to keep walking."

Cassie practically skipped down the tree-lined street. It was a perfect plan. Though of course she didn't know exactly how they would lead Bushy Eyes to Trexler's house. Or what it would take to convince Bushy Eyes that the astronomer was an alien. Or how they would have time to do all these things with the science fair less than a month away. Still—it was a great plan, all the same, and Cassie felt her confidence growing.

But nothing, absolutely nothing, could have prepared Cassie and Zeke for what they saw when they reached the field. Grant Trexler, cast and all, was standing at the edge of the clearing, talking a mile a minute and gesturing toward the open ground with his good arm. Standing next to him, soaking in every word and gesture, was Ben O'Brien.

CHAPTER

10

"What the . . . ?" Cassie exclaimed, looking frantically at Zeke. The Triminican stood motionless, his eyes glued to Ben.

"Zeke?" Cassie nudged him with her elbow.

"The spy academy never prepared me for this," groaned the alien.

"Let's go," Cassie whispered.

"Where?" Zeke said out of the side of his mouth.

"Anywhere. My house," said Cassie.

But it was too late. Side by side, Grant Trexler and Ben O'Brien walked toward them.

Cassie tried to act as casual as possible.

"Hi, Ben," she said. "I see you have a new friend."

"At least my new friend's human!" said Ben, an evil glint in his eye.

Cassie thought fast. "Are you sure?" she asked.

Ben looked confused for a second. Then he sort of laughed.

"So," said Zeke, trying to imitate Cassie's casual air. "Where did you two meet?"

"That's the funny thing," said Ben. "Mr. Trexler here was waiting for me outside the school today. He said he got information about the kid who cheated in the fight."

"I did not cheat!" said Zeke, offended.

Ben went on as though he didn't hear. "Mr. Trexler said he had something to show me."

"And that something was?" asked Cassie. Her heart was thundering in her ears so loudly she could barely hear herself speak.

"Stop beating around the bush!" snarled Trexler, looking straight at Zeke. "Where's the ship?"

"I am sorry if you have lost your ship, sir, but I do not have it," said Zeke. "By the way, how did you injure your arm?"

Cassie laughed.

Grant laughed, too. But it was an evil, raspy laugh, and it made Cassie shudder.

Grant moved in front of Zeke, so close that their noses almost touched. "I know about you," he said, menacingly. "And I just want you to know that I am your enemy. I *will* find your ship and that weirdo dog of yours. That's a promise!"

Zeke didn't flinch. He didn't move a muscle. He just said, "Ben, your new friend seems very upset. Perhaps you should take him home."

"I'm not going anywhere until I see the spaceship!" Grant spat out the words, the veins on his neck throbbing.

"If you are so positive that I am an alien, why not just capture me?" asked Zeke.

"You know why not," snarled Grant. "I can't prove anything without seeing the ship or that—that creature of yours."

"Well," said Zeke. "Then you are out of luck." He turned to Cassie. "It is time for us to be getting home. Your parents will be waiting for us."

"Yes, of course," said Cassie, catching on.

"This ain't the way to your house, Cassie. I know where you live," said Ben.

"We were just taking a walk before going home to do our schoolwork," said Cassie. "Ben, you should be home, too, thinking about our science project."

Ben's mouth dropped open. "Since when do you care about the science fair?" he asked.

"Come on, Ben," said Cassie. "You know I've always liked you. And you're really good in science. It will be fun."

"You have? I am? It will?" stammered Ben.

"Sure," said Cassie. "Bye, now."

She grabbed Zeke's arm, and without another word the two spies headed down the street in the direction they had just come from. As they walked, Cassie took a few deep breaths. Her legs were still shaking and her palms were sweaty.

"You were great," she said to Zeke.

The Triminican didn't answer. Cassie looked over at her friend and saw that most of the color had drained from his face.

"It'll be okay, Zeke," she said. "We have a plan."

Cassie and Zeke went straight to Cassie's house. They lingered in the kitchen long enough for Cassie to introduce Zeke to her mother. Then they grabbed a snack and locked themselves in Cassie's bedroom. They needed time to think.

"Why would Trexler think Ben could help him?" Cassie asked.

"I do not know. But you said he saw the fight. So he must know Ben holds a grudge against me. He probably asked Ben to snoop around."

"He must be desperate to ask Ben for help," said Cassie.

"Maybe Ben is not as stupid as everyone thinks," said Zeke.

They ate their snacks without speaking, trying to figure a way out of their newest dilemma.

The silence was broken by a knock at the door.

"Cassie?" called Mrs. Williams. "There's a phone call for Zeke. A Marilee Tischler."

Zeke groaned. "What now?" he said.

"Thanks, Mom," Cassie called. Then she looked at Zeke. "You'd better take it," she whispered.

While Zeke was downstairs, Cassie tried to figure out what to do about Ben. By the time he returned, she had an idea.

"What did Marilee want?" she asked.

"She wants to meet with me tomorrow about the science fair."

"What did you tell her?"

"I told her okay. What else could I say?"

"Nothing, I guess," said Cassie sadly. Then her face lit up. "Hey, I think I figured out what to do about Ben. Did you see the look on his face when I asked him if he was sure Grant was human?"

"Sure. It was the same look he always has on his face," said Zeke.

"No it wasn't, Zeke," said Cassie. "He looked really confused. Like he didn't know who to believe."

"So?"

"So what if we can convince him that Trexler really *is* an alien."

"And then," said Zeke, catching on, "we can use Ben to lead that spy right to Trexler!"

Cassie nodded eagerly. "Think about it. It's perfect. Trexler will think Ben is helping him out, and if we do it right, old Bushy Eyes will never get a chance to see you or me or Spot!"

Zeke's eyes sparkled.

"I think you may have something here, Cassie," he said. "Only, how are we going to get Ben to help us?"

"That's a really good question, Zeke. Unfortunately, I don't know the answer yet."

Zeke looked out the window of Cassie's bedroom. The sun was beginning to set. He rose from his seat on the floor and stretched.

"It is getting late," he said. "And we both know if Spot gets too worried about where I am, he will come looking for me. I had better get back."

"Okay," said Cassie. "We can figure out the rest of this tomorrow." Suddenly an awful thought crossed her mind. "Zeke, you don't have any materializer disks with you. How are you going to get back to the ship?"

"I could borrow that two-wheeled vehicle of yours," Zeke said hopefully.

"You mean my bicycle?" said Cassie. "I don't

think so, Zeke. People might notice you riding across the field. Besides, it takes practice to ride a bicycle."

"Then I suppose I will have to walk. I just hope I get back before that overprotective robot goes out looking for me."

"I know what you mean," Cassie said, laughing. "He's worse than my mother."

"Meet me at school tomorrow morning," said Zeke. "We can finish the plan then."

"I'll be there," said Cassie. "Half an hour before the first bell."

As Cassie watched Zeke walk away from her house, she had a funny feeling that something was wrong.

CHAPTER

11

Cassie woke with a start, sat up in bed, and looked around the darkened room. The clock on her nightstand glowed 3:00 A.M. Something had awakened her. A loud noise. What was it?

She jumped when she heard the banging sound again.

It was coming from the window. Cassie leapt out of bed and pulled up the shade, then slapped her hand across her mouth to keep from screaming. It was Zeke. But he looked awful. He was scratched and filthy, and his clothes were torn. The wig covered only half of his head, flopping down over his right ear but leaving bare skin on the left side.

"Oh no!" Cassie cried softly. She raised the window quickly and helped her friend inside. "Zeke, what happened?"

"The ship is gone!" said Zeke. "I've been looking for it ever since I left here."

"What do you mean? I don't understand," said Cassie.

"It was not where we left it," said Zeke. "I thought perhaps Spot had moved it. I ran all over the field, and I kept deactivating the invisibility shield, hoping to find it."

"Why would Spot move the ship?" asked Cassie.

"I do not know," moaned Zeke, sitting down and putting his head in his hands. "Mirac and Inora will be furious. We are stranded here without the ship."

Cassie paced the room, deep in thought. "This doesn't make sense, Zeke. Spot wouldn't just move the ship."

"He would if he thought he was protecting it from being discovered," said Zeke. "He is programmed to protect."

"How would he move it?" asked Cassie.

"The same way Mirac moved it," said Zeke. "By throwing materializer disks."

"Or maybe," said Cassie, thinking hard, "maybe he would do what we did in the field that day. You know, make the ship hover fifty feet above the ground!"

"Perhaps," said Zeke.

"But that's it! Don't you see?" Cassie said,

pacing back and forth. "That's where Spot put the ship. You just need to point that invisibility shield deactivator up!"

"Sorry, Cassie," said Zeke, yawning. "I have already thought of that. These small pocket deactivators do not have that large a range. You have to be right next to the ship."

Cassie looked at her friend. He looked pale and exhausted. She walked over to her closet and rummaged inside, finally pulling out what she was looking for.

"What's that?" asked Zeke.

"This," said Cassie, "is a sleeping bag." She rolled it open on the floor and pulled a pillow down from her bed. "Get some sleep, Zeke. We'll find your ship in the morning."

Zeke smiled and dove into the sleeping bag. Cassie heard soft snores the second his head hit the pillow. She set her alarm clock for half an hour before her parents usually woke up. Zeke would need a shower in the morning.

Zeke was too tired to talk on the way to school the next day. And he kept falling asleep in class. Cassie was awake enough, but Ben O'Brien was driving her crazy. Every time she looked over at him, he was staring at her and grinning. In social studies class, he passed her a note. Cassie slid it into her history book. If she had to leave the room to go to the principal's office, Zeke would be left alone.

By the time the last class of the day began, Cassie was busy thinking of ways she could convince her parents to let Zeke spend the night. It would be difficult. They always insisted on speaking with the parents of a friend who was sleeping over. But she would have to think of something. There was no telling how long it would take to find the ship.

She was staring out the window of her English class, deep in thought, when she saw someone motioning to her from outside. She squinted to see better, and the huge head and hairy body came clearly into sight. Spot!

Cassie rubbed her eyes. When she looked again, Spot was gone. Cassie shot up her hand and asked to be excused to go to the bathroom. The teacher looked at the classroom clock and frowned, but allowed her to leave the room.

Spot was waiting in the bushes outside. Crouching next to him, Cassie whispered, "Where have you been? Where's the ship? Zeke looked all over for you! I thought you were programmed to protect him."

"I am also programmed to protect the ship," droned Spot.

"I know, I know," said Cassie. "But you should protect Zeke more than you protect the ship."

"I will explain," said Spot.

"Then explain," said Cassie impatiently.

"The man was back, and he was getting too close," said Spot.

"Which man?"

"The man with the white plaster on his arm," said Spot.

"Trexler!" said Cassie. "But I still don't understand. Where's the ship?"

"The spaceship is where it has always been," said Spot. "Only fifty feet higher."

"I knew it!" said Cassie. "But why didn't you find Zeke after you brought it down?"

"It is not down," said Spot simply.

"What? Why not?"

"It is stuck."

"What?" repeated Cassie, a little louder this time.

"The apparatus that lowers the ship has malfunctioned. The ship is locked in place at fifty feet above the planet's surface. When the fuel runs out, it will crash to the ground. Fuel will run out in four hours, thirty-two minutes."

"What? Oh my . . . I have to get Zeke," said Cassie. She glanced at her watch. She had been out of the classroom for eight minutes.

"Spot, I have to get back into class. But school will be over in fifteen minutes. Wait here for us. Don't move. Don't do anything. Okay?"

"Where is Zeke?"

"We'll *both* be out here in fifteen minutes."

Cassie raced back to class. She tried to get Zeke's attention, but he was asleep again, his eyes open, staring straight at the blackboard. When the bell rang, he came awake with a start.

Cassie sprang to his side.

"Spot's outside!" she whispered.

Zeke's face lit up. But before he could say a word, Marilee Tischler appeared, the usual sickly-sweet smile on her face.

"Ready, Zeke?" she said.

"For what?" asked Zeke numbly.

"You haven't forgotten our meeting this afternoon?" asked Marilee. "For the science fair? Remember?"

"Zeke isn't feeling well," Cassie said quickly. "You'll have to meet with him another time."

"How come you always answer for him?" Marilee snapped.

"Don't be ridiculous, Marilee," said Cassie. "Look at him. Doesn't he look sick?"

Marilee studied Zeke's ripped clothes and puffy face.

"We-ell," she simpered. "He *has* looked better."

"We can meet tomorrow instead," Zeke said, taking his cue from Cassie and speaking in a weak, pained voice.

Marilee sighed. "I suppose that would be all right," she said.

Zeke and Cassie watched her flounce off.

"Now we can go," said Zeke, stifling a yawn.

"Not yet," said Cassie. "Let's wait here until everyone's gone. We don't want Spot to be seen."

As they waited for the area to clear, Cassie told Zeke everything she had learned from Spot. When she repeated the part about the ship being stuck, Zeke suddenly sprang awake.

Zeke started yelling the second he saw Spot.

"What is wrong with you? You are supposed to be able to fix any malfunction that occurs on the ship!"

"Zeke, lower your voice," Cassie whispered urgently, glancing around the seemingly empty school yard.

Zeke took a deep breath and glared at the robot. "I suppose you forgot to bring materializer disks," he said a bit more quietly.

Spot produced a golden disk from a panel on his side.

"And the coordinates?" Zeke asked sternly.

"They are preset!" Spot reported.

When they materialized on board the ship, Cassie ran to the window. Once again the field was fifty feet below.

"Zeke, what are you going to do?" she asked softly, turning around.

Zeke was standing at the far end of the control panel, talking to Spot. "Why did you use the manual control?" he said testily.

"Standard procedure," responded Spot.

"There is no standard procedure for temporarily suspending a ship in the air!" Zeke snapped.

"Rule 3026 in the *Intergalactic Defense Manual* states that 'no procedure that threatens to reveal the location of a ship shall be instituted at any time,'" droned Spot.

"What does that have to do with your having used the manual control?" Zeke yelled.

"The manual control is effective for quietly raising a ship up to fifty feet," Spot explained.

"So?"

"Nonmanual control necessitates engaging the ship's main engine."

"SO?" Zeke sputtered.

"It is noisy," Spot said simply.

Zeke was silent. He just stared at the robot. Spot stared back. After a moment, Zeke spoke softly.

"Are you saying that the other time we raised the ship, it was done manually so no one would hear the main engine starting up?"

"Affirmative," said the robot.

"Well. Then I guess I am sorry for yelling at you. I guess it *was* standard procedure."

"No apology is necessary," droned the robot.

"What?" said Zeke. "Oh, of course." He turned to Cassie, grinning. "I have been listening to you talk about the robot having feelings so much that I started to believe you."

Cassie smiled thinly.

"What are we going to do, Zeke?" she asked again.

"We are going to turn on the main engine and lower the ship!" Zeke announced. "Robot, deactivate the manual control."

"That is not advisable," said Spot. "The ship will begin to descend immediately."

"I will engage the main engine the second we are off manual control," said Zeke.

"But . . ."

"We have no alternative. What are we going to do—wait until we run out of fuel completely and crash? Do it!"

"Deactivating manual control," said the robot. He punched a series of flickering lights on the control panel.

"Accomplished!" he announced.

Cassie felt her feet drop out from beneath her as the ship plunged down to the earth. She screamed and grabbed on to the control panel as Zeke flew past her in the air.

"Hit the main switch, Cassie," Zeke yelled as he crashed into a wall.

Cassie looked frantically at the control panel. There were hundreds of buttons and switches and knobs. Which was the main switch?

"Ten seconds until impact," said Spot.

The ship lurched to the side. Cassie lost her grip on the control panel and fell to the floor.

"Five seconds until impact."

"Hit it now!" screamed Zeke, trying to crawl up the tilted floor of the ship toward Cassie.

"Three seconds until impact!"

Cassie saw it. A bright orange switch larger than the flickering buttons around it. In a single motion she pulled herself up and lunged for the switch.

"One second until . . ."

There was a whine and then a roar. The ship lurched and rattled. Cassie slid across the floor down to where Zeke was trying to get to her.

Then, suddenly, they were going up. The sound of the engines thundered in Cassie's ears, drowning out even the thumping of her heart.

As soon as the ship leveled off, Zeke raced to the control panels and sprang into action. Skillfully, he lowered the ship to the ground. Then he shut off the main engine, and all was still.

Finally, Zeke spoke.

"I am going to sleep," he said.

While Zeke slept, Cassie and Spot sat on cushiony clouds of light in the sitting room and plotted. By the time Cassie left the ship, an extra stack of materializer disks in her pocket, they had come up with a plan. They would tell Zeke all about it tomorrow.

"The first part was Spot's idea," Cassie explained the next morning. Zeke was well rested, and the two spies and the robot were once again in the ship's main room.

"It came to him when I explained what the cast on Grant Trexler's arm was for."

"Stupid invention," Spot muttered.

"I agree," said Zeke. "Whoever heard of immobilizing an arm just because of a broken bone?"

"That's what Spot said!" Cassie exclaimed. "He said the way you treat broken bones on your planet is to shoot—uh . . ."

"Barticulum rays," said Spot.

"Right. Barticulum rays at it."

"Which heals the bones instantly," added Spot.

"So?" said Zeke.

"So," Cassie said, her eyes glowing. "That's how we're going to convince Ben O'Brien to help us."

"I missed something," said Zeke.

"Think about it," said Cassie. "Trexler already told Ben when and how he broke his arm. If we fix Trexler's arm and Ben sees him without a cast less than a week after he broke it, Ben's sure to think there's something strange going on. We can convince him that Trexler is an alien!"

"Do you really think Ben is that stupid?" asked Zeke.

"Yes!" cried Cassie and Spot at the same time.

"Well, okay. What's the rest of the plan?" asked Zeke.

"Once we can convince Ben to help, there will be no risk of Bushy Eyes ever seeing us. Spot has already set up the computer so Bushy Eyes's magnetic field variable detector will send him straight to Trexler's house, where one of us will have planted some Triminican gadgets. We throw Trexler to the spy, and we're rid of them all!"

"But what about Ben?" asked Zeke. "What if he tells everyone that Trexler is an alien and we helped capture him?"

"So what?" asked Cassie. "No one's going to believe him."

"I like it!" said Zeke. "When do we start?"

"How about now?" asked Cassie.

The two spies put on their spy belts, stuffed materializer disks in their pockets, and prepared a ray gun full of barticulum. Cassie waited while Zeke lectured the robot on not moving the ship, not doing anything at all, in fact, until they returned. Then Cassie and Zeke materialized outside Grant Trexler's house. As they touched down on the ground, Cassie realized they had forgotten one very important detail.

"Zeke, what about the cast?" she asked as Zeke stared up at the house, trying to determine if the astronomer was home.

"What do you mean?" asked Zeke.

"We have to get it off his arm before we use the barticulum ray. Otherwise, Ben will never see that the arm is fine."

Zeke groaned. "How are we going to do that?"

"We could tackle him to the ground and saw it off," said Cassie. Even as she said it, she knew it was a bad idea.

"I guess we will have to wait until tonight, when he is asleep," said Zeke.

"Oh, great," said Cassie. "Like he won't wake up when we break into his bedroom and start sawing at his arm."

"We will not have to saw, Cassie," said Zeke. "We can dissolve the plaster with zorcanian 6."

"I thought that was a metal dissolver," said Cassie.

"It is," explained Zeke. "But do you not think that something that dissolves metal can dissolve plaster, too?"

"I don't know," said Cassie. "What do you think?"

"I think it is worth a try," said Zeke.

"I sure hope he's a sound sleeper," said Cassie.

At five after midnight, Cassie and Zeke melted the doorknob on the front door and slipped inside the astronomer's house. They moved swiftly, sticking exactly to the schedule they had made earlier that day.

The bedroom was on the second floor. Grant Trexler was snoring so loudly they could hear him downstairs.

Cassie kept an eye on the staircase while Zeke planted the Triminican devices they had selected for framing Trexler. To be safe, Spot and Zeke had decided on gadgets that would probably be invented on Earth within the next fifty years. They chose no weapons.

"Okay, we can go," Zeke whispered to Cassie when he was finished. They climbed the stairs and stood outside the snoring man's room.

"What are we going to do if he wakes up?" Cassie mouthed.

Zeke shrugged his shoulders and opened the door. The spies slipped inside.

The moon was shining brightly outside the bedroom window, shedding enough light for Cassie and Zeke to see the sleeping form in the bed. The astronomer slept on his back, the broken arm above the covers. In the moonlight, the white plaster looked almost fluorescent. Cassie kept her eyes on Grant's sleeping face while Zeke went to work.

The zorcanian 6 melted the plaster quickly—too quickly. In an instant there was a huge puddle of melted white ooze all over the bed.

Grant moaned in his sleep.

"Hurry!" whispered Cassie.

Zeke slipped the barticulum-filled ray gun out of his pocket and flipped a small switch. Working quickly, Zeke shot the barticulum rays up and down the injured arm. There was a constant hum from the gun as he worked. It was a low, soft sound. But it was loud enough. Grant Trexler's eyes flew open.

Cassie screamed.

"You!" roared Trexler.

Zeke jumped back. Grant sprang from his bed and lunged at the alien.

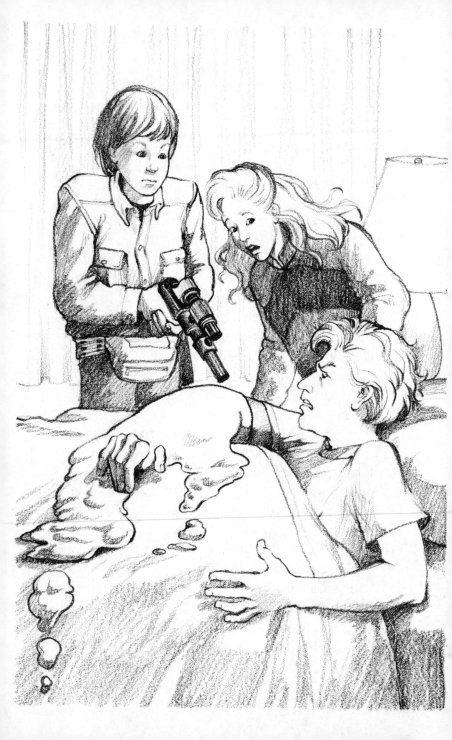

Zeke and Cassie ran out of the bedroom, a screaming Grant Trexler hard on their heels. The two spies raced through the house and out the front door, then down the street and around the corner. The astronomer followed, shouting threats as he ran. He was fast. But the two spies were faster, and they gained enough distance to duck behind a darkened house. As the raging man gained on them, Zeke threw a materializer disk, and he and Cassie disappeared into the night.

CHAPTER

Cassie slept late Sunday morning. After breakfast, she decided to spend a couple of hours
doing her homework before joining Zeke on
the spaceship. She had been neglecting her
schoolwork lately, and since there was no way
of knowing how long Zeke would remain on
Earth, she figured she should get back in the
habit of studying. Fifth grade was hard enough
as it was. She didn't want to repeat it next
year.

Halfway through a particularly difficult math
problem, Cassie realized she had completely
forgotten about the next step in the plan. She
raced down the stairs and headed straight for
the phone in the kitchen. Too bad there wasn't
a phone on the spaceship. It would have been
easier for Zeke to disguise his voice for this
call.

After three rings, Ben O'Brien picked up. "Yeah?" he said.

Cassie covered the mouthpiece with a dish towel and lowered her voice.

"Ben O'Brien?" she said huskily.

"Yeah? Who's this?"

"Just think of me as a friend. This is a warning."

"What? Who is this?" Ben barked in Cassie's ear.

"This is an anonymous phone call," Cassie said into the dish towel. "Grant Trexler is an alien. Stay away from him. He's been telling you lies."

Cassie slammed down the receiver before Ben could say another word. Her heart was thumping so loudly she was afraid it was going to jump out of her throat. She took several deep breaths and steadied herself. This was no time to fall apart. There was far too much to do today.

Phone call number two. Cassie waited ten minutes and called Ben back. This time, she used her own voice.

"Hi, Ben. It's Cassie."

"Yeah?"

"Do you want to meet today to discuss the science fair project?" Cassie asked as nicely as she could.

"Really?"

"Sure. We have to get started, don't we? Meet me at the school playground at one o'clock."

"Don't you want to come over here?" asked Ben.

"No!" snapped Cassie. "I mean—it's a beautiful day. Let's meet outside by the swings."

For a split second, Cassie thought Ben was going to ruin the whole plan.

"Uh, okay," he said.

"See you there," Cassie said quickly, and hung up before Ben could change his mind.

The hardest phone call was still ahead. Cassie practiced her Ben O'Brien voice several times before dialing. The phone rang four times. Then an answering machine clicked on.

"Hello. You have reached the home of Grant Trexler. Leave a message after the beep."

"Yeah, uh," Cassie grunted in her best Ben O'Brien voice. "This is Ben O'Brien. I've got information for you about you-know-what. Meet me at the school playground at one-fifteen."

By the time Cassie finished her math homework, told her parents she was meeting a friend about the science fair, and materialized on board the ship, it was twelve-thirty.

"Where have you been? We have trouble," Zeke said the moment he saw her.

"More than we had yesterday?" asked Cassie.

"Much more," said Zeke. He was standing next to Spot at the window of the ship. The robot's eyes were glued to something outside.

"Look!" said Zeke, pointing out the window.

Cassie looked. "Bushy Eyes!" she gasped. "I guess he got his money."

The spy was combing the area around the ship with his magnetic field variable detector.

"So what's the problem?" asked Cassie. "We have the frequency, don't we? Send him away, Spot."

"I think we should wait until after you meet with Ben," said Zeke. "We don't want Bushy Eyes getting to Trexler's house too soon."

Cassie glanced at her watch.

"I've got to go," she said. She peered out the window and watched the spy snooping closer and closer. "But listen, Zeke, I really think you should send him to Trexler's house now. It will start things rolling. And there's no way Trexler's not going to meet us at the playground." If he gets the message on his machine, she thought but did not say.

"I suppose you are right," said Zeke. "Very well, Spot, activate the field detector. And make sure the coordinates are correct."

Spot moved to the computer console and punched in a series of numbers. A map came up on the screen, a blinking light targeting

Grant Trexler's house. The robot slid to the other end of the control panel and flipped a switch. A high-pitched whine filled the room, and just as Cassie covered her ears to block out the sound, Spot activated another switch on the console. Cassie uncovered her ears and watched out the window.

At first, there was no change in the man's behavior. He continued his search around the ship, consulting the device in his hand every few seconds. Then, suddenly, Bushy Eyes looked confused. He stood motionless in the field, staring at the detector in his hand. He moved a few steps toward the ship, peered at the device, then moved a few steps away and checked again. Turning away from the ship, he looked up into the sky. Slowly but surely, he moved farther and farther away from the invisible spaceship, his eyes turned upward the entire time.

"It's working!" Cassie gasped in delight.

"Of course," said Zeke, grinning.

"He thinks the ship is moving," said Spot.

The three of them continued to watch until the man disappeared from sight, his face bobbing up and down over and over again as he looked from the device in his hand to the sky above.

CHAPTER

14

Ben was hanging upside down on the jungle gym when Cassie reached the playground. He grunted when he saw her, pulled himself into a sitting position, and jumped off clumsily, landing in the dirt. Cassie bit the inside of her cheek to keep from laughing.

"You're late!" said Ben, standing up and heading straight for the swings.

"Sorry," said Cassie, following him.

They each sat on a swing, saying nothing. In all the years she had known him, Cassie couldn't remember saying more than a few words to Ben. She couldn't imagine why Ms. Grayson had teamed them together for the science fair. But for the moment, at least, that didn't matter.

When Cassie finally spoke, she tried to sound as casual as possible. She figured Ben should be pretty easy to trick.

"So, Ben, how have you been?"

"Okay, I guess," said Ben suspiciously, kicking at a clump of earth beneath his feet.

"How's your new friend?"

"I knew it!" said Ben. "I knew you didn't want to meet about the science fair."

Cassie shifted gears quickly. "Look, Ben. You and I both know that my cousin *isn't* an alien."

"Do we?" asked Ben. "Then why'd that guy find me and tell me what he told me?"

"What?"

"That astronomer guy. Why would he say Zeke's an alien if he isn't?"

For a second, Cassie was too surprised to answer. Ben was actually behaving as if he had a brain.

"Ben," she said cautiously, "did it ever occur to you that maybe Mr. Trexler is the alien?"

"Well," said Ben thoughtfully, "he is kind of strange."

"Well, he *is* an alien," said Cassie. "And Zeke and I found out about it. We've been gathering evidence to show to important people. When we have enough, we're going to turn him in."

"What kind of evidence?"

"I can't show that to you right now. You'll just have to trust me."

"Why?"

"You'll just have to, Ben. This man is dangerous. I just wanted to warn you. He has . . ." Cassie paused for dramatic effect. "Powers!"

"What kind of powers?"

"Well, for one thing, he has this ability to always know where we are. I bet he knows we're here talking about him right now."

"Really?" said Ben doubtfully. "And what other powers does he have?"

"You'll just have to watch him carefully and see for yourself," said Cassie. "He's very tricky," she added.

"Did you call this morning and warn me about him?" Ben asked.

"What? No!" Cassie lied. "Why would I do that?"

Ben shrugged. "Someone called."

"See!" said Cassie. "I'm not the only one who knows he's an alien."

Ben was thinking about this when a car pulled up to the front of the school. Grant Trexler got out.

"Look!" said Cassie, pointing. "I told you he'd find us."

Ben's mouth dropped open. "Cassie, look at his arm!" he practically shrieked.

"What about it?" asked Cassie, innocently.

"The cast is gone!"

"Wow!" said Cassie. "That's amazing. When I broke my foot last year, the cast had to stay on for six weeks. Didn't he break his arm last week?"

"When did you break your foot?" asked Ben. "I don't remember you wearing a cast last year."

"Uh, it was over the summer," said Cassie, thinking quickly.

As Grant Trexler reached the playground, Cassie felt a rush of excitement race through her body. The plan was working perfectly. Ben would ask about the astronomer's arm, and when Trexler told him that Zeke and Cassie had snuck into his house in the middle of the night and fixed it, she would roll her eyes and say, Sure, we like you so much we just had to fix your arm. There was no way Ben would believe Trexler's story. It was perfect!

The astronomer loomed over the two children sitting on the swings. He said nothing. He just stood glaring down at them.

"Uh, hi!" said Ben.

"What's she doing here?" snarled Grant, scratching at the coat sleeve covering his once-broken arm.

"We're meeting about a school project," said Ben. "What are *you* doing here?"

"You know very well what I'm doing here!" Grant snapped.

"What happened to your arm?" asked Ben.

Cassie held her breath. This should be good.

"Oh, this," said the astronomer, waving his once-injured arm around. "That stupid doctor made a mistake. He put the cast on before the X rays came back. It turned out it wasn't broken, only sprained. So he took the cast off yesterday." He stopped swinging the arm and scratched at it again.

Cassie almost fell off her swing. With all of the planning Zeke, Cassie, and Spot had done, this possibility had never occurred to them.

"Where's your little alien friend?" Grant asked Cassie.

"I don't know what you're talking about," said Cassie. "None of my friends are aliens. What do you want, anyway?"

"My business is with Ben. Why don't you leave us alone," said Grant.

"Or what?" said Cassie.

The astronomer glared at her. Cassie couldn't think of anything else to say. She was about to get up off the swing and leave when Grant scratched at his arm again.

"Does your arm itch?" she asked. "You keep scratching it." Before Grant could stop her, Cassie reached out and pushed up the sleeve of his coat. The astronomer jumped back, and the sleeve fell into place again. But not before both Cassie and Ben had seen the purplish glow that surrounded his arm.

"Your . . . your arm!" cried Ben. "It's glowing!"

"Don't be ridiculous," sputtered Grant Trexler.

"Then let us see it again," said Cassie. She was so excited she could hardly sit still.

"I have more important things to do than sit around talking to two stupid children!" the astronomer said. He turned on his heels. Still scratching at his arm, he went back to his car and drove away.

Cassie looked at Ben. His mouth was wide open and his eyes were almost popping out of his head.

CHAPTER 15

Zeke was waiting for them in the food court of the mall as planned. Ben stared suspiciously at the Triminican, but took a seat and waited for him to speak.

"I am glad Cassie could convince you to help us," said Zeke.

"She didn't," said Ben. Zeke looked at Cassie for an explanation.

"Ben didn't believe me at first," Cassie said carefully. "But then Grant Trexler showed up at the playground."

"Really?" said Zeke, playing along. "He just keeps showing up wherever we are, it seems."

"Yeah, he sure does!" said Ben.

"His arm is out of the cast," Cassie told Zeke. Zeke pretended to be surprised.

"So soon?" he said. "That is strange."

"Not as strange as the color of his arm," said Ben.

Zeke looked at Cassie out of the corner of his eye. "What color *is* his arm?" he asked.

"It's purple!" exclaimed Ben. "Not only that—it glows!"

This time Zeke was genuinely amazed.

"I wonder why!" he said.

"It's just like Cassie said," stated Ben. "Grant Trexler is the real alien."

"And that is what convinced you to help us?" Zeke asked.

"Maybe," said Ben. "It depends what you want me to do."

Zeke reached into his pocket and pulled out a golden metal object. It was a suphenphone and had been carefully picked by Zeke and Spot for exactly this purpose. Of all the devices belonging to the Triminicans, this was one of the few that would not put them in danger if its use was discovered. Zeke placed the suphenphone on the table and slid it over to Ben.

"What is it?" asked the bully.

"We do not know," said Zeke. "But it dropped out of Trexler's pocket one of the days he was chasing us."

Ben grabbed the metal device and studied it. He punched at a series of buttons and the suphenphone began to quake. A shrill, quivering noise pierced the air. Cassie covered her ears. Frantically, Ben punched at the buttons until the noise died out. Zeke smiled to himself. He was quite fond of Altoonian opera. But when he had played it for Cassie, she had the same reaction Ben had just had. The music was unbearable to human ears.

"He really is from another planet," Ben said softly.

"Will you help us expose the alien?" asked Zeke.

"That depends," said Ben, still fingering the suphenphone. "You haven't said what you want me to do."

"We want to you to give this to a man who will capture Grant Trexler," said Cassie.

"Why can't you give it to him yourself?" asked Ben suspiciously.

"Because," Cassie said slowly. "This man is very dangerous. And Trexler has already told him that Zeke is the alien. If one of us gives this to him and tells him it's Trexler's, he won't believe us. He'll just think it belongs to Zeke."

"Who is this man?" asked Ben.

"He's a man who captures aliens for the government," said Cassie, just as she and Zeke had rehearsed.

"Really?" said Ben. "There are other aliens running around?"

"Oh, yes," said Cassie. "Lots. But this man captures them before anyone else finds out about them."

"It is part of a secret government project," Zeke added to the story.

"The man came to town looking for Trexler," said Cassie. "But Trexler was too smart for him and put him on Zeke's trail to throw him off."

"I see," said Ben.

"So? Will you help us?" asked Cassie.

Ben thought about it for a minute. "Will you pay me?" he finally asked.

"Pay you?" cried Cassie. "How much?"

Ben looked straight at Zeke. "Teach me karate," he said.

Zeke studied the boy carefully. Ben was a whole lot brighter than most people gave him credit for.

"You are saying that if I teach you karate you will help us?" Zeke asked.

"That's what I'm saying," said Ben.

"And you'll never tell anyone what you've done for us?" asked Cassie.

"Why not?" asked Ben.

"Well, for one thing," said Zeke, "if Grant Trexler ever finds out what you have done, he might escape and take revenge."

"And there's no knowing what awful things that man could do," Cassie added.

Some of the color drained out of Ben's face. For a second, Cassie thought that they had gone too far. If Ben was too scared, he might back out on them.

"Are you scared, Ben?" she asked.

"Me? Scared? Never!" said Ben.

"Then is it a deal?" said Zeke.

"Deal," said Ben.

"Deal," said Cassie.

They shook hands all around. Then Cassie and Zeke told Ben exactly what they wanted him to do.

When Cassie and Zeke arrived back on board the ship, Spot was watching Bushy Eyes searching outside the ship with his magnetic field variable detector.

"What's he doing here?" cried Cassie. "I thought we got rid of him."

"He's gone back and forth between the ship and that astronomer's house three times," Spot explained. "Although we have transported the ship's magnetic signature to a spot directly above Trexler's house, he suspects his detector has malfunctioned."

"That is okay," said Zeke. "We are ready for him now. The next time he returns to Trexler's house, our friend Ben will be waiting for him."

"I wish we could listen to what happens inside the house," said Cassie.

"We can!" said Zeke, grinning. "I planted a microphone in the bookcase when we were there before."

"Zeke, you're brilliant!" said Cassie. "Let's go. I wouldn't miss this for the world."

"Absolutely not!" said Spot. "You are not to go near that house while both of those dangerous men are there."

"Relax, Spot," said Cassie. "We're just going to watch and listen from across the street. No one will see us. Besides, we need to be there in case anything goes wrong."

"In the event something does go wrong, what precisely would you do?" asked Spot.

Cassie shrugged and looked at Zeke. Zeke shrugged back. They had no idea.

They waited on the ship until Bushy Eyes, shaking his head in confusion, headed back out of the field. Then they materialized in the small park across from Grant Trexler's house. The astronomer's car was in the driveway.

"I just hope he's home," said Cassie.

"We will check," said Zeke. The two spies huddled together, sharing the earphones to the listening device hidden in Trexler's house.

"Oh no. He is not alone!" Zeke exclaimed.

"Can you hear those other voices?"

Cassie listened carefully. Suddenly her face lit up. "That's the TV, Zeke. I recognize the show."

"Look!" Zeke pointed down the street. Right on schedule, Ben O'Brien walked slowly toward the house.

"I really hope he doesn't blow it," Cassie whispered.

Ben looked at a piece of paper in his hand and then peered at the numbers on the houses as he walked.

"He couldn't even memorize the address," Cassie groaned.

"Here comes Bushy Eyes," said Zeke.

Sure enough, the man was approaching, staring down at the field detector in his hand and muttering to himself. Cassie held her breath and watched as Ben moved slowly toward him.

"We should have bugged Ben, too," Cassie whispered to Zeke.

"Shhh. Watch," said Zeke.

They watched as Ben walked up to the man and blocked his path. The man looked startled and swiftly slipped the device in his hand into a coat pocket.

Ben spoke to the man.

The man spoke back.

Ben spoke again and gestured at Grant Trexler's house. Then he pulled the suphenphone out of his pocket and handed it to Bushy Eyes. The man examined the metal device, turning it over and over again in his hands. For the first time since Cassie and Zeke had been dealing with Bushy Eyes, they saw the spy smile.

Ben turned to leave, but Bushy Eyes grabbed his arm. Cassie and Zeke watched in fear as the two spoke back and forth, more and more excitedly. Suddenly the man dropped his arm, and Ben disappeared down the street.

"It worked!" gasped Cassie.

"I just hope Ben did not say anything stupid," said Zeke.

"I'm telling you it worked," Cassie repeated. "Look! He's going inside."

Mr. Bushy Eyes Kolnikov, spy and alien hunter, pushed open the door of the astronomer's house and slipped inside.

CHAPTER

At first the only sounds they heard were the voices from the television set. After a few moments, even those fell silent. For a full minute, Cassie and Zeke heard nothing inside the astronomer's house. Then there was a crash.

"Who's there?"

Silence.

"I said, who's there?"

Cassie squeezed Zeke's hand and listened. They could hear the sound of footsteps.

"Freeze!"

"What the. . . ?"

"I said, freeze!"

"Look, if this is a robbery, take anything you want, just don't hurt me," said Grant.

"What a wimp!" Cassie whispered to Zeke.

"Move!" snarled Bushy Eyes.

"What do you want?"

"Sit down. I want to look around."

Cassie and Zeke could hear muffled sounds through the earphones as the man searched the house.

"Aha! What exactly is this?"

"I . . . I have no idea," said Grant.

"And this strange object? What is this?" asked Bushy Eyes.

"Hey! What the heck is going on here?"

"Remove your shirt!" demanded the spy.

"What? Why?"

"Just take it off!"

"Okay, okay."

Zeke and Cassie grinned at each other. This was the moment they were waiting for.

"That's a strange color for an arm, isn't it?" snarled Bushy Eyes.

"It's those kids," Trexler protested.

"Kids?" said Bushy Eyes. "I don't know what you're talking about!"

"Look," said Trexler, "I don't know who you are or what you want. But there's an alien from another planet in this town. It's a kid. And I'm really close to capturing him. This is all his stuff."

"Sure it is," repeated Bushy Eyes. "And I suppose he made your arm turn purple and glow, too."

"That's right," said Grant.

"Look here," growled Bushy Eyes. "The only kid I know is some snot-nosed boy who couldn't possibly be an alien. Get up—we're leaving!"

"What? Why? Who are you?"

"Grant Trexler, you are an alien from another planet. And I have been hired to capture you. I followed you from your ship's hideaway five days ago. Then, when you noticed me, you moved your ship. You've got it hidden somewhere up there."

"What?" shouted Grant. "I do not!"

"Shut up! You're behaving like a child. I must admit that I'm disappointed. I had somehow hoped you were from a superior race of beings. Now move!"

The astronomer started yelling so loudly that Cassie had to hold the headphone away from her ear. "You're making a big mistake! I'm telling you that kid is an alien. He planted this stuff. He did this to my arm. You've got to believe me. I'll cut you in on the capture. Please. Stop. You're hurting me. Let go. This isn't fair. . . ."

Cassie and Zeke watched as the front door to the house flew open and Grant Trexler emerged, one arm twisted behind his back by Bushy Eyes.

"I wonder where he's taking him?" Cassie whispered.

She didn't have to wait long to find out. Bushy Eyes glanced up and down the street to make sure no one was watching. Then he pushed the astronomer into Grant's car.

"Yippee!" cried Cassie, as the car pulled away.

"Let us celebrate!" shouted Zeke.

"When do I get my first karate lesson?" said a voice behind them.

Cassie and Zeke turned together. Ben O'Brien stood there grinning.

"Ben! When did you get here?" asked Cassie.

"Just now," said Ben. "I was waiting down the street and saw the car drive off. I figured you two were around here somewhere."

"Ben, you were great!" said Zeke.

"I know," said Ben.

"I have an idea," said Cassie. "Let's go to the mall and get the biggest ice cream sundaes we can find. My treat!"

"*Then* can I have a karate lesson?" asked Ben.

Zeke laughed.

"Yes, Ben. You have definitely earned it!"

As they headed toward the Hillsdale Mall, Cassie felt as if a huge weight had been lifted from her shoulders. There had been entirely too many spies snooping around the last few weeks. And entirely too many problems to deal with. With Grant Trexler and Bushy Eyes gone, life could get back to normal.

Of course, she would still have Ben O'Brien as a science fair partner. But maybe that wouldn't be so bad after all. And there was still the matter of Zeke being stuck on planet Earth . . . and Mirac and Inora were still in Hawaii . . . and the principal still wanted to meet Zeke's parents. But for two expert spies like Cassie and Zeke, there was no problem too big to overcome. Cassie and the spy from outer space were an unbeatable team!

About the Author

Debra Hess has done a fair amount of spying in her life, and is pretty sure that a few of her friends are from outer space. The author of several popular books for young readers, she lives in Brooklyn, New York, with her husband, a lot of fish, and two newts.